For my Father and Grandfather – PS

Phaidon Press Inc.
65 Bleecker Street
New York, NY 10012

Phaidon Press Limited
Regent's Wharf
All Saints Street
London N1 9PA

phaidon.com

First published 2018
© 2018 Phaidon Press Limited
Text and illustrations copyright © Paul Schmid
Typeset in Radiant Bold

ISBN 978 0 7148 7724 2
002-0718

Printed in China

Little Bear Dreams

Paul Schmid

Φ

Of what do little bears dream?
Bright snowflakes, perhaps...

or dark starry nights.

Hot chocolate...

cold pizza.

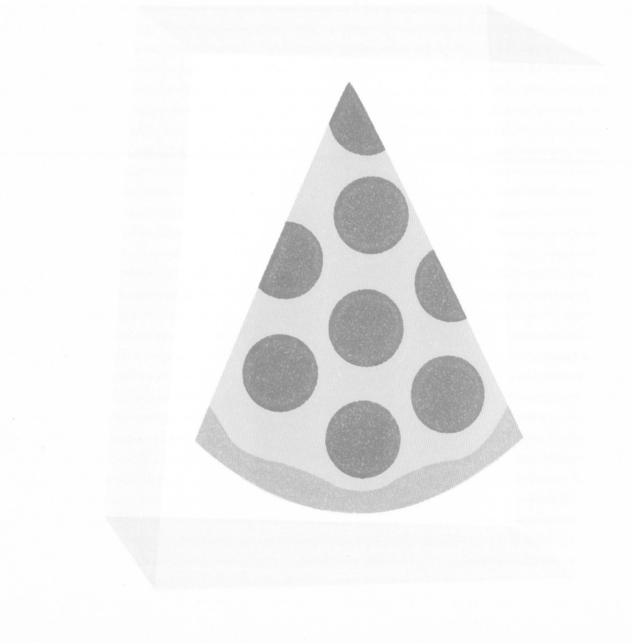

Straight horizons...

and curly moustaches.

Hide-and-seek.

Big love...

small friends.

Blue water...

blue skies...

blue ice.

Short tails...

and tall hats.

Soft, snowy beds.
Warm fur...

and frosty nights.

Good night
my Little Bear.